How to Grow a Friend

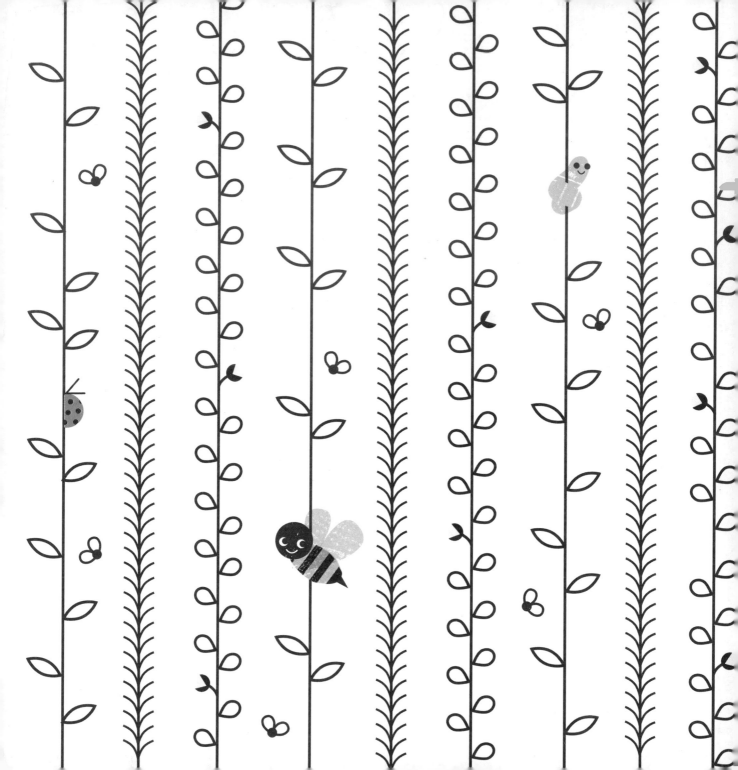

For Riley:
A fine farmer, and friend
—S.G.

No part of this publication may be reproduced, stored in a retrieval system,
or transmitted in any form or by any means, electronic, mechanical, photocopying, recording,
or otherwise, without written permission of the publisher. For information regarding permission,
write to Random House Children's Books, a division of Penguin Random House LLC,
1745 Broadway, New York, NY 10019.

ISBN 978-1-338-17270-6

12 11 10 9 8 7 6 5 4 3 2 1   17 18 19 20 21 22

Printed in the U.S.A.   40

First Scholastic printing, February 2017

Book design by John Sazaklis

How to Grow a Friend

by Sara Gillingham

SCHOLASTIC INC.

To grow a friend,

first plant a seed in good soil.

A friend needs water . . .

warm sunshine . . .

and space to bloom.

To grow a friend, talk

and listen.

It doesn't happen overnight.

Sometimes a friend bugs you.

To grow a friend,

chase the bugs away
together!

And don't let your friend
get stuck in the weeds.

If a friend is drooping,

do something sweet.

Good friends stand by each other in rain

or shine.

Good friends
make things brighter.

To grow a garden of friends,

remember that new buds can sprout . . .

in surprising places!

And there is always room
for one more.

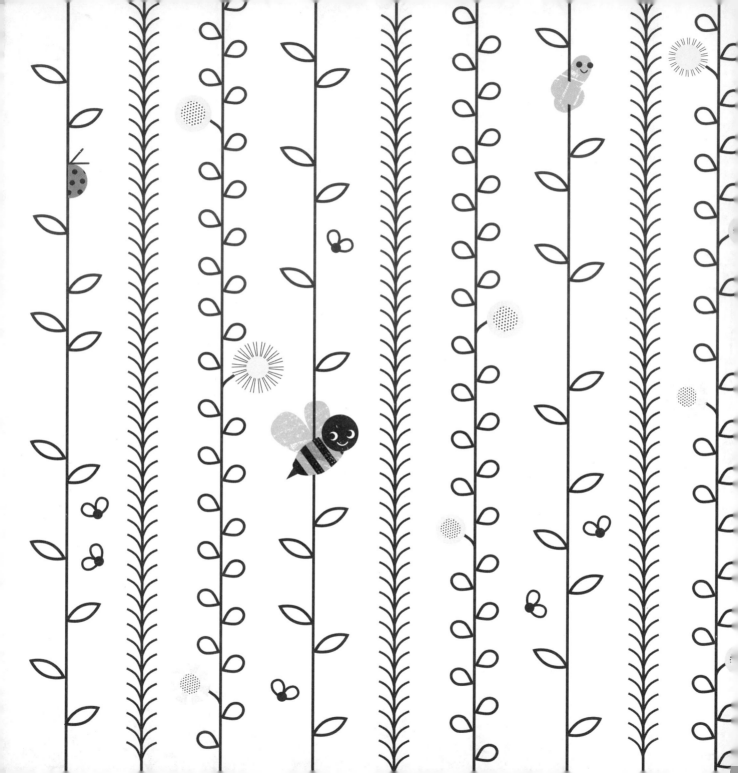

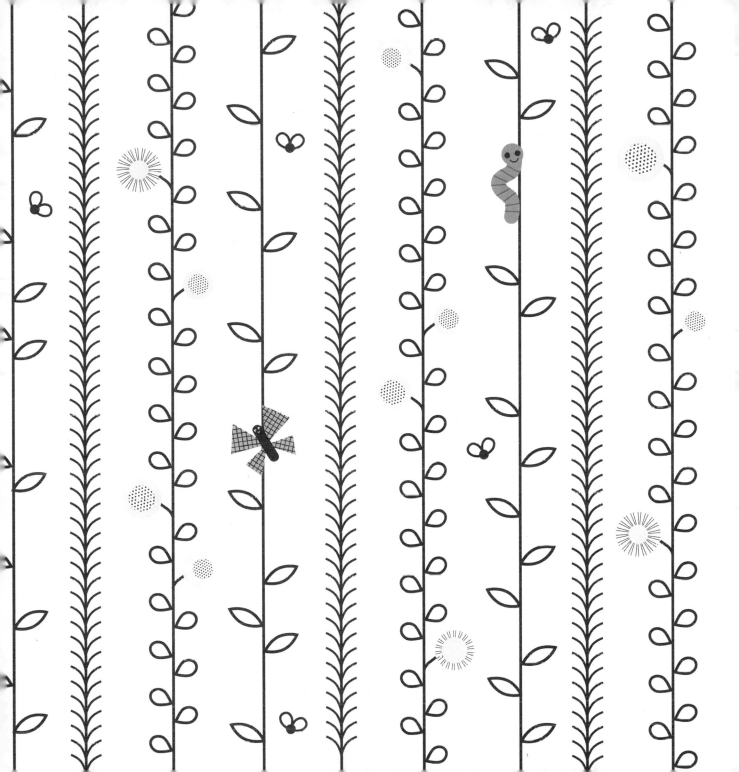